Yannick Grotholt – Writer
Comicon – Artist

New York

LEGO® CHIMA Graphic Novels Available from PAPERCUTZ™

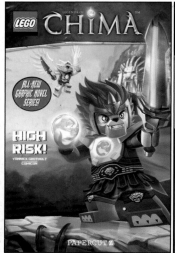

Graphic Novel #1
"High Risk!"

Graphic Novel #2
"The Right Decision"

Graphic Novel #3
"CHI Quest!"

LEGENDS OF CHIMA
#3 "CHI Quest!"

Yannick Grotholt – Writer
Comicon – Artist
(Miguel Sanchez – Pencils
Marc Alberich – Inks
Oriol San Julian – Color)
Bryan Senka – Letterer
Alexander Lu – Editorial Intern
Beth Scorzato – Production Coordinator
Michael Petranek – Editor
Jim Salicrup
Editor-in-Chief

ISBN: 978-1-62991-076-5 paperback edition
ISBN: 978-1-62991-077-2 hardcover edition

Printed in Canada
October 2014 by Friesens Printing
1 Printer Way
Altona, MB R0G 0B0

Papercutz books may be purchased for business or promotional use. For information on bulk purchases please contact Macmillan Corporate and Premium Sales Department at (800) 221-7945 x5442.

FSC
www.fsc.org
MIX
Paper from responsible sources
FSC® C016245

LEGO LEGENDS OF CHIMA graphic novels are available for $7.99 in paperback, $12.99 hardcover. Available from booksellers everywhere. You can also order online from Papercutz.com. Or call 1-800-886-1223, Monday through Friday, 9-5 EST. MC, Visa, and AmEx accepted. To order by mail, please add $4.00 for postage and handling for first book ordered, $1.00 for each additional book and make check payable to NBM Publishing. Send to: Papercutz, 160 Broadway, Suite 700, East Wing, New York, NY 10038.

LEGO LEGENDS OF CHIMA graphic novels are also available digitally wherever e-books are sold.

Papercutz.com

Distributed by Macmillan
First Papercutz Printing

LAVAL

THE **CRAWLERS** MAY BE CONQUERED FOREVER, BUT TREACHEROUS SABER-TOOTHED TIGERS, MAMMOTHS, AND VULTURES HAVE BEEN STRIKING TERROR INTO THE HEARTS OF CHIMA'S INHABITANTS. THE **ICE HUNTER TRIBES** CAN FREEZE ANYTHING AND ANYONE INTO ICE.*

CHI QUEST!

*SEE LEGENDS OF CHIMA SEASON 3!

BUT THERE IS HOPE: THE **PHOENIX TRIBE**, WHO LIVED INSIDE **MOUNT CAVORA** FOR MILLENNIA, HAVE PROMISED TO GIVE **LAVAL** AND HIS FRIENDS THEIR SUPPORT. BUT LAVAL HAS DOUBTS ABOUT THE RELIABILITY OF HIS NEW ALLIES...

I DON'T TRUST THOSE FIRE BIRDS, **CRAGGER**. FIRST THEY LEAVE US TO FIGHT THE SCORPIONS ON OUR OWN AND NOW THEY SUDDENLY WANT TO MAKE **ERIS** A PHOENIX?

CLANG

THE PHOENIXES ARE THE OLDEST TRIBE IN CHIMA! YOU SHOULDN'T DISTRUST THEM.

I'M COMING WITH YOU! CHIMA'S DESTINY IS MY BUSINESS, TOO.

AS YOU WISH.

WHERE ARE YOU OFF TO, ERIS?

KING LAGRAVIS HAS FORBIDDEN US TO TRAVEL THROUGH CHIMA ALONE. THE BLIZZARDS ARE TOO DANGEROUS.

DON'T WORRY. I AM UNDER THE PROTECTION OF THE PHOENIXES. THEY HAVE INVITED ME ON A TOUR OF **PHOENIX CITY** AND WANT TO SHOW ME THEIR PALACE!

WHAT?! WHY WASN'T **I** INVITED?!

IN THE MEANTIME, THE GORILLAS ARE PREPARING FOR THE **GREAT MELLOW**. FOR THE FIRST TIME, GORZAN IS PERMITTED TO UTTER THE HOLY WORDS-- OR TO BE MORE PRECISE, THE HOLY WORD.

DUUUUUUUUUDE!

SUDDENLY, SNOW STARTS FALLING...

FEEL HOW THE **TOWER FLOWER** IS CARRYING YOU AWAY FROM HERE!

...SABER-TOOTHED TIGER **SIR FANGAR**...

...**VARDY** THE VULTURE... AND **MAULA** THE MAMMOTH...

WILL YOU LOOK AT THAT BEAUTIFUL FLOWER! I WISH I COULD CAPTURE THE SIGHT OF IT FOR ALL ETERNITY.

NEITHER GORZAN NOR THE OTHER GORILLAS HAVE NOTICED THAT THEY ARE BEING WATCHED BY THE LEADERS OF THE ICE HUNTER TRIBES...

"HOLD ON A MINUTE," SIR FANGAR SAYS, **"I CAN!"**

SECONDS LATER, THE TOWER FLOWER AND THE GORILLAS ARE COMPLETELY FROZEN...

TING

A MASTER-PIECE!

IN THE MEANTIME, ERIS AND LAVAL HAVE REACHED THE PHOENIX TEMPLE...

FLUMINOX, THE KING OF THE PHOENIXES, AND HIS LOYAL SERVANT TORMAK ARE ALREADY EXPECTING ERIS...

MY DEAR ERIS. HOW DELIGHTFUL THAT YOU ACCEPTED OUR INVITATION.

WE ARE HONORED TO WELCOME YOU HERE IN OUR HALLS.

WUMP

I'M FINE! THANKS FOR ASKING.

COME, THERE IS MUCH TO SEE.

WHAT THE HECK--?!

BUT LAVAL IS NOT PUT OFF THAT EASILY. HE DID NOT SPEND MONTHS LIVING IN THE OUTLANDS FOR NOTHING!

THOSE VINES WON'T STOP ME-- BUT THEY WILL DELAY ME!

THE ARCHITECTURE OF LION CITY IS ALREADY PRETTY IMPRESSIVE. BUT IT IS NOTHING COMPARED TO THE IMPOSING STRUCTURES OF THE PHOENIXES...

FINALLY! I MADE IT THROUGH!

I COULDN'T HELP HEARING THE *BIG* WELCOME CELEBRATION IN HONOR OF ERIS!

THERE'S QUITE A CROWD! EVERY ROW IS PACKED!

EXCUSE ME... COULD I JUST... SORRY...

‡GRRRRRR!‡

A KING'S SON IN THE BACK ROW. IF MY FATHER EVER FOUND OUT ABOUT THIS...

8

9

PERFECT. AS LONG AS THEY'RE BUSY WITH THEIR IGLOO, THE WAY IS CLEAR FOR US.

BUT THE ICE HUNTER TRIBES HAVE SENSED THE YOUNG HEROES...

BEWARE. THREE *WARM-BLOODS* ARE HIDING SOMEWHERE NEARBY. AND ONE OF THEM IS A *PHOENIX.*

A PHOENIX? I'VE ALWAYS WANTED TO HAVE A PHOENIX ICE SCULPTURE. *STEALTHOR*, KEEP YOUR EYES PEELED!

YOU CAN RELY ON IT, SIR FANGAR.

AN I-I-ICE SCULPTURE?

DON'T WORRY. IT WON'T COME TO THAT.

GUYS?

THE FIRE CHI ISN'T FIRE CHI AT ALL! IT'S A PAINTED ROCK!

CHIMA. SINCE THE ARRIVAL OF THE *ICE HUNTER TRIBES*, ICY WINDS AND FREEZING TEMPERATURES HAVE PREVAILED HERE...

SAVED IN THE NICK OF TIME

SIR FANGAR, THE LEADER OF THE SABER-TOOTHED TIGERS, DOES NOT QUITE SEEM TO HAVE GOTTEN OVER HIS LAST DEFEAT AT THE HANDS OF *LAVAL* AND HIS FRIENDS...

HOW COULD YOU ICE-MUPPETS ALLOW A TINY BIRD TO MAKE *FOOLS* OF YOU?

WHAT'S AN *ICE-MUPPET?*

WHO CARES?! WHAT I NEED TO KNOW IS--

WHAT'S A RULER FROM CHIMA WITH EIGHT LETTERS. *LAVERTUS?*

HMM. OR *CROMINUS...*

I NEED A NEW TROPHY FOR MY SCULPTURE COLLECTION. MOVE YOUR BACKSIDE AND BRING ME A *WARM-BLOOD!*

WHO? ME?

YES, YOU, *VORNON.* OF ALL THE GOOD-FOR-NOTHING VULTURES, YOU ARE THE *WORST!*

MEANWHILE, NOT VERY FAR AWAY, INSIDE THE *PHOENIX TEMPLE, KING FLUMINOX* AND THE OTHER PHOENIXES HAVE SPENT DAYS DISCUSSING THEIR STRATEGY IN THE FIGHT AGAINST THE ICE HUNTER TRIBES WITH *LAVAL, CRAGGER,* AND *ERIS...*

KNOW YOURSELF AND KNOW YOUR ENEMY.

FIRST WE MUST GATHER INFORMATION ABOUT THE *ICE FORTRESS* BEFORE WE CAN THINK ABOUT AN ATTACK.

SIRE, IT WOULD ALL BE SO MUCH EASIER IF THE TRIBES OF CHIMA FINALLY GOT *FIRE CHI--*

LOOK! OUTSIDE! FLINX!

HE'S BEING ATTACKED BY A *VULTURE!*

TORMAK! PUT A TEAM TOGETHER IMMEDIATELY AND GO AFTER THEM.

DO NOT WORRY, MY KING. I WILL BRING FLINX BACK HOME.

TORMAK--CRAGGER AND I WILL JOIN YOU! WHAT ABOUT YOU, ERIS?

ERIS WILL STAY HERE AND COMPLETE HER TRAINING TO BECOME A PHOENIX.

WE CANNOT ALLOW HER TO BE PUT IN HARM'S WAY AGAIN.

*B*UT BEFORE LAVAL LEAVES...

TAKE THIS CHI, JUST IN CASE. BUT DON'T LET KING FLUMINOX KNOW ABOUT IT!

FASTER! WE MUST NOT LOSE HIM!

WHY ARE THE PHOENIXES BEING SO COY?

WE LIONS ARE BRAVE WARRIORS. WE HAVE *EARNED* THE FIRE CHI!

THAT IS NOT FOR ME TO JUDGE.

YOU MUST SPEAK TO KING FLUMINOX.

WE SHOULD PROCEED WITH CAUTION.

FROM THIS POINT WE ARE IN THE REALM OF THE...

...ICE HUNTERS.

20

I'M WARNING YOU-- MY FATHER WILL TURN YOU INTO A **PUDDLE!**

BUT FIRST I WILL TURN YOU INTO AN *ICE SCULPTURE.*

THEN MY COLLECTION WILL FINALLY BE COMPLETE.

THE FRIENDS ARE PUTTING THEMSELVES IN **EXTREME DANGER** IN ORDER TO RESCUE FLINX...

WE NEED A PLAN AS QUICKLY AS POSSIBLE.

WHAT ABOUT ERIS'S FIRE CHI?

CAREFUL, LAVAL-- WHATEVER YOU DO, NOT--

OOPS!

--DROP IT!

ANY OTHER IDEAS?

22

QUICK, GRAB FLINX AND RUN FOR IT. I WILL KEEP THE SABER-TOOTHED TIGERS AT BAY.

⸰BRRR⸰ ICE IS EVEN WORSE THAN WATER!

HEY! I THOUGHT WE WERE GOING TO PLAY ANOTHER ROUND?

MAYBE NEXT TIME. I'M AFRAID IT'S FLINX'S BEDTIME.

HI, GUYS! BYE, VORNON!

STAY WHERE YOU ARE, LITTLE PUSSYCATS!

HOW MANY MORE TIMES? I'M A *CROCODILE*, NOT A *PUSSYCAT*!

WE MUST SHAKE THEM OFF SOMEHOW. QUICK--*INTO THE WOODS!*

THEY MUST HAVE GOTTEN PAST TORMAK! THEY'RE RIGHT BEHIND US!

I'M RUNNING AS FAST AS I CAN!

KEEP RUNNING! WE'RE ALL OUT OF--

"--LUCK!"

CHOOM

KKRAK

CRRACCK

FIRE! RUN FOR YOUR LIFE!

I DON'T BELIEVE IT! FIRE--

THERE'S NOTHING THE SABER-TOOTHED TIGERS FEAR MORE THAN REAL FIRE--!

DON'T GET YOUR HOPES UP TOO SOON, WARM-BLOODS!

WE WILL SEE EACH OTHER AGAIN, THAT I PROMISE YOU!

CRRASSHH

WHAT'S WRONG, FLINX? YOUR FATHER IS WAITING FOR US TO BRING YOU HOME.

BUT WHAT ABOUT TORMAK?

I'M AFRAID THERE'S NOTHING MORE WE CAN DO FOR HIM.

27

SON!

FATHER!

I PROMISE TO NEVER RUN AWAY FROM HOME AGAIN.

HEART-WARMING, ISN'T IT?

I HATE TO ADMIT IT, BUT IT IS!

IF CRAGGER AND I HAD HAD FIRE CHI, WE COULD HAVE STOOD BY TORMAK AND DEFEATED THE SABER-TOOTHED TIGERS!

VERY WELL. IF YOU PROVE TO BE *WORTHY*, I WILL GIVE YOU FIRE CHI.

WHERE ARE YOU GOING NOW, MY SON?

TO THE ARMORY! I'M GOING TO GET MYSELF A SWORD AND RESCUE TORMAK!

DIDN'T YOU JUST PROMISE YOUR FATHER NEVER TO RUN AWAY AGAIN?

TORMAK! HOW DID YOU GET HERE?

HAVE I GOT A STORY FOR YOU...

THE END.

28

CRAGGER

BEHOLD-- THE LEGENDARY **PHOENIX TEMPLE**, HOME TO **KING FLUMINOX** AND THE OTHER PHOENIXES, WHO HAVE GUARDED THE PRECIOUS FIRE CHI FOR THOUSANDS OF YEARS...

CRAGGER IN THE COOLER

THESE *TRIALS* OF KING FLUMINOX'S SEEM TO *NEVER END*, CRAGGER!

DON'T COMPLAIN, LAVAL! YOU SAID YOU WANTED TO PROVE YOURSELF A WORTHY BEARER OF THE *FIRE CHI!*

I'M LOSING MY *G-GRIP--!*

AHHHHH!

ME TOO!

≥OOF!≤

NO! WE FAILED *AGAIN!*

WE'LL *NEVER* REACH THE FIRE FLOWER LIKE THIS! WHAT WE NEED IS WINGS.

CRAGGER BETTER APPRECIATE WHAT I'M DOING FOR HIM!

LAVAL...

THE CROCODILES... THEY HAVE JOINED FORCES WITH SIR FANGAR!

*BUT THINGS AREN'T ALWAYS WHAT THEY SEEM. THE TRUTH IS THAT **CROOLER** IS ONLY CONCERNED ABOUT HER BROTHER. SIR FANGAR'S PLAN SEEMS TO BE WORKING...*

AND WILL YOU REALLY LET CRAGGER FREE IF MY TRIBE ALLIES ITSELF WITH YOU?

YOU HAVE MY WORD. NOW WILL YOU SIGN THE AGREEMENT?

I DON'T KNOW. I STILL NEED SOME TIME TO THINK.

DON'T HESITATE FOR TOO LONG, MY CROCODILE PRINCESS.

FLUMINOX

SOON...

I'M FLABBER-GASTED THE ICE HUNTERS DIDN'T EVEN TRY TO FOLLOW ME!

HA! ALL *TEETH* AND NO *BITE!*

LAVAL ARRIVES IN CHIMA, BUT SENSES SOMETHING WRONG WITH HIS FRIENDS...

COME ON, GUYS! AREN'T YOU READY FOR THE MOST THRILLING *SPEEDORZ* TOURNAMENT OF ALL TIME?!

WHAT'S WRONG? YOU LOOK LIKE YOU JUST SPENT A WEEKEND IN THE *OUTLANDS!*

LAGRAVIS HAS CANCELLED THE RACE. THERE ISN'T ANY *GOLDEN CHI* THIS MONTH BECAUSE THE CHI POOL HAS *FROZEN OVER!*

THEN WE'LL JUST USE MY *FIRE CHI* AS THE PRIZE!

45

48

54

WATCH OUT FOR PAPERCUTZ™

Welcome to the thrilling, totally-tantalizing third LEGO® LEGENDS OF CHIMA graphic novel, by Yannick Grotholt and Comicon, from Papercutz—those humble humanoids dedicated to publishing great graphic novels for all ages. I'm Jim Salicrup, the Earth-bound Editor-in-Chief—not to be confused with the Editor-with-CHI! We've got a lot to talk about, so let's get right to it!

When we're not working away on creating great graphic novels at our palatial Papercutz offices, chances are we're probably at a comicbook convention somewhere, trying to get the word out about such graphic novels as LEGO LEGENDS OF CHIMA, LEGO NINJAGO, ANNOYING ORANGE, and many others. Probably the biggest convention every year has to be Comic-Con International: San Diego, better known as the San Diego Comic-Con. Papercutz has been exhibiting at this colossal comic-con since we published our very first graphic novels back in 2005, and it's always fun to meet both current and future Papercutz fans. Of course, we're eager to attract as many LEGO fans as possible too, after all LEGO exhibits at Comic-Con as well. Usually all it takes is displaying the latest LEGO LEGENDS OF CHIMA and LEGO NINJAGO graphic novels at our booth, and LEGO fans immediately take notice. We also run episodes from the animated LEGO LEGENDS OF CHIMA and LEGO NINJAGO TV series, and have often had fans stand in front of our TV monitor completely transfixed—sometimes even mouthing every line of dialogue along with the show! This is even more incredible than it sounds because you wouldn't believe how much other media is vying for fans' attention at these cons.

But every now and then we're surprised when an unexpected guest drops by our booth, and this year we were honored to have none other than the LEGO Group's own Tommy Andreasen stop by. Tommy had flown in to San Diego especially to appear on several of the LEGO Group's panels, telling fans exactly what to expect from the LEGO Group in 2014, 2015, and beyond. Somehow, Tommy was able to wend his way through the crowded Comic-Con corridors and make his way through to our booth! He's one of the big creative guys at the LEGO Group, involved with "Concepts & Stories," and had a big role in developing LEGO LEGENDS OF CHIMA, so we were truly honored that he came by to see us!

From Left to Right: a Rabbid, John Cena, Jim Salicrup, Tommy Andreasen, and Michael Petranek. [Photo by Cherie Tieri.]

Tommy checks out the LEGO LEGENDS OF CHIMA graphic novel. [Photo by Cherie Tieri.]

To be perfectly clear, we're excited to meet everyone who visits us at conventions. It's so great to actually meet the people we're creating these graphic novels for, and to hear their feedback. We can easily get swept up by all the work that's involved in putting these books together, that's it's great to be reminded that there are people out there as excited as we are about them.

Speaking of which, we better get back to work! Now we have to start putting LEGO LEGENDS OF CHIMA #4 together! Think there's a CHI for that?

Thanks,

JiM

STAY IN TOUCH!

EMAIL: salicrup@papercutz.com
WEB: papercutz.com
TWITTER: @papercutzgn
FACEBOOK: PAPERCUTZGRAPHICNOVELS
FAN MAIL: Papercutz, 160 Broadway, Suite 700, East Wing, New York, NY 10038